This edition published by Parragon Books Ltd in 2016

Parragon Books Ltd
Chartist House
15–17 Trim Street
Bath BA1 1HA, UK
www.parragon.com

Copyright © 2016 Disney Enterprises, Inc.

Illustrated by the Disney Storybook Artists

ISBN 978-1-4748-8429-7

Printed in China

Disney
M☉ANA

PaRRagon
Bath · New York · Cologne · Melbourne · Delhi
Hong Kong · Shenzhen · Singapore

Moana was a little girl who lived with her family on the island of Motunui. Her home was a beautiful place, surrounded by a coral reef and shimmering blue seas.

Her father, Tui, was the chief of the island. Moana was destined to be chief too, one day.

Chief Tui cared very much about his people and made sure they were happy and safe. He didn't allow anyone to sail beyond the coral reef, where it might be dangerous.

After all, Motunui had everything the villagers needed. Who would ever want to leave?

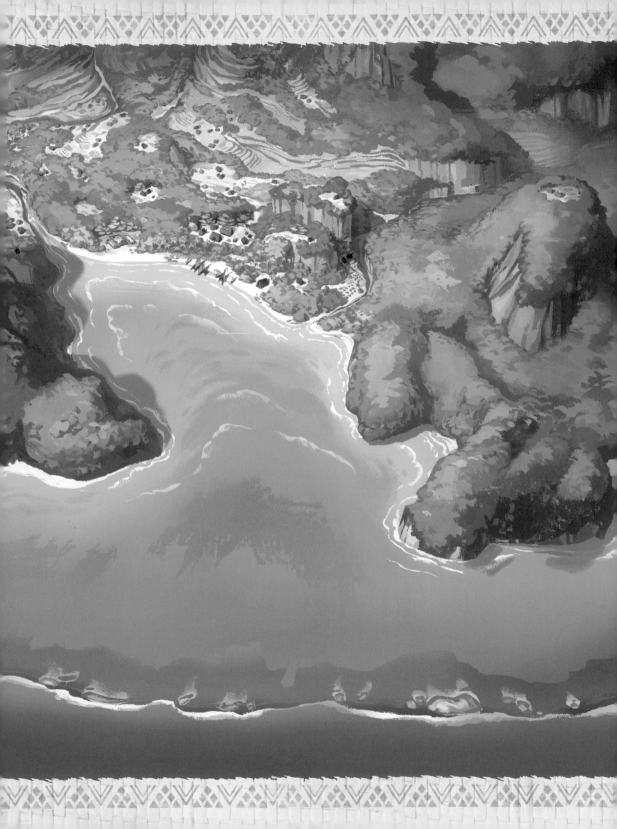

One day, Moana's Gramma Tala was telling a story to the children in the village.

"Long ago, there was an island goddess called Te Fiti," she began. "All life sprang from her heart. But one day, the giant demigod Maui took her heart. As Maui made off, a fire demon called Te Kā attacked him and the heart was lost to the sea forever."

The children were terrified – all except little Moana, who loved her grandma's stories.

Later that day, Moana was playing by the sea when
the seawater magically rose up around her. She saw
a spiral stone in the water and grasped it.

Just then, Chief Tui came looking for his
daughter. As he picked up Moana, she dropped
the stone.

Gramma Tala had been secretly watching
from the bushes. She picked up the
spiral stone before a wave
washed it away.

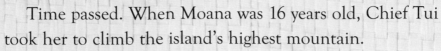

Time passed. When Moana was 16 years old, Chief Tui
took her to climb the island's highest mountain.

"One day, you will add your stone to this mountain,"
he said, "and raise our whole island higher."

Tui told Moana how important it was for her to stay in the village and lead her people. Moana wanted to make her father proud, but she couldn't help wondering what might be out there, beyond the coral reef.

Later that day, Gramma Tala took Moana to a
secret cave. Moana couldn't believe her eyes – the
cave was filled with sailing boats! The boats belonged
to their ancestors, who had been voyagers.

Gramma Tala explained that after Maui stole Te Fiti's heart, darkness took over the seas. The ancient chiefs stopped Moana's people from sailing to keep them safe.

"The darkness will spread to our island too, unless someone finds Maui and takes him to restore Te Fiti's heart," said Gramma Tala, "and the sea chose you." She gave the spiral stone to Moana. It was actually the heart of Te Fiti!

Soon after, Gramma Tala passed away. With her last breath, she told Moana to find Maui.

Moana took a little boat from the cave and set sail. But soon, a storm rose up. A giant wave crashed into her boat and everything faded to black.

When Moana woke up, she was on a strange beach.

Suddenly, Maui appeared. Moana had landed on his island!
Moana asked Maui to help her restore Te Fiti's heart, but he
refused – he wanted to find his magical fishhook instead. The
hook gave him the power to shape-shift into different animals,
and he'd lost it in his battle with Te Kā. Maui trapped Moana
in a cave and took her boat to go and search for his hook.

Moana was determined not to let Maui get away. She escaped from the cave and dived into the sea just as Maui set sail.

Suddenly, the sea pulled Moana under the water and placed her on the boat!

"You will put back the heart!" Moana said in her bravest voice, holding the spiral stone out to him. But Maui still refused to help her.

As Moana and Maui argued, spears started landing around them.
They were being attacked by the Kakamora – little coconut-clad bandits.

Both Maui and Moana fought back against the tiny pirates until they
were able to sail away.

Maui was impressed by Moana's bravery. He finally agreed to go
with her to find Te Fiti, but said they would never succeed without
his shape-shifting powers. They needed to find his fishhook first.

Maui was pretty sure who had his hook – Tamatoa, a giant crab who loved to collect treasures. Tamatoa lived in Lalotai, the realm of the monsters. By the next morning, Moana and Maui had reached the tall, rocky island that was the entrance to the realm.

The friends climbed up the steep rock and finally reached the peak. Moana and Maui each took a deep breath and jumped into the pitch-black hole that led into Lalotai.

In another world under the ocean, Moana and Maui found
themselves in a huge, dark cavern.

Suddenly, Moana saw the hook, hidden in
a pile of treasures. But just then, the ground
rose up to reveal Tamatoa, who pinned Maui
to the ground.

Thinking quickly, Moana held out
the stone from her necklace.

Tamatoa scrambled to snatch the stone – he couldn't resist new treasures. Moana grabbed the hook, but then dropped the stone as she and Maui escaped.

"But – the heart!" cried Maui.

"He can have it, I've got this one," Moana whispered, as she opened her hand to reveal the real heart of Te Fiti. Moana had tricked Tamatoa with an ordinary rock!

Before the monster could attack, a geyser exploded underneath the two friends, launching them out through the top of the realm.

The pair travelled onwards to find Te Fiti. They were nearly
there! But as they approached the island, Te Kā suddenly
appeared out of a cloud of ash. Maui transformed himself into
a hawk using his hook, but Te Kā knocked Maui from the sky.

Moana caught Maui in her boat and headed back towards Te Fiti. Maui tried to stop her: "We won't make it! Moana, turn back."

Te Kā's fist slammed downwards to crush their boat, but at the last second, Maui changed himself back into his human form and raised his hook to block Te Kā's fist.

A huge wave swept Moana, Maui and the boat far away. Moana wanted to go back, but Maui refused. Te Kā's blow had cracked the demigod's precious hook. Maui turned into a hawk again and angrily flew off.

Moana spoke to the sea with tears in her eyes. "I couldn't make it. You'll have to choose someone else," she said, heartbroken. Then she held the heart out to the sea and a wave reached up and took it back.

Just then, the spirit of Gramma Tala appeared and said that she would always be with Moana, whatever she decided to do.

Suddenly, hundreds of ghostly canoes emerged from the sea, and a chorus of voices rose up. "Know who you are," the voices chanted. They were the spirits of Moana's voyaging ancestors.

Moana realized that she would be the one to restore Te Fiti's heart. She dived over the side of her boat and took the heart back from the sea bed.

Back on her boat, Moana headed towards Te Fiti once again. Te Kā wanted to stop her. But just before Te Kā struck Moana, Maui appeared out of nowhere to take the blow!

While Maui and Te Kā battled on, Moana reached Te Fiti. But something was terribly wrong: the island was just an empty crater, and the goddess was nowhere to be seen.

Te Kā swooped down in front
of Moana, but the demon no longer
seemed frightening. Trusting her
instincts, Moana reached out and
placed the heart into Te Kā's chest.
She watched as the face of the lava
monster transformed. Now that the
goddess's heart was restored, she
was changing back to her true self.

Te Fiti opened her hand to
reveal Maui's hook, fixed – she had
forgiven him. Te Fiti's island exploded
with flowers and came back to life,
at last.

Back on Motunui, Tui was very worried about his
missing daughter. But then Moana appeared on the
horizon, and Chief Tui and the villagers of Motunui
were overjoyed.

Moana had restored Te Fiti's heart, which meant her people could sail safely across the sea again, just as they had done long ago.

Moana finally knew who she was – the next great explorer, destined to lead her tribe on amazing new adventures.